Ruby, Valerie and Louise were practising for the Bunny Scout Concert.
Their group was called Ruby's Red Hot Trio.

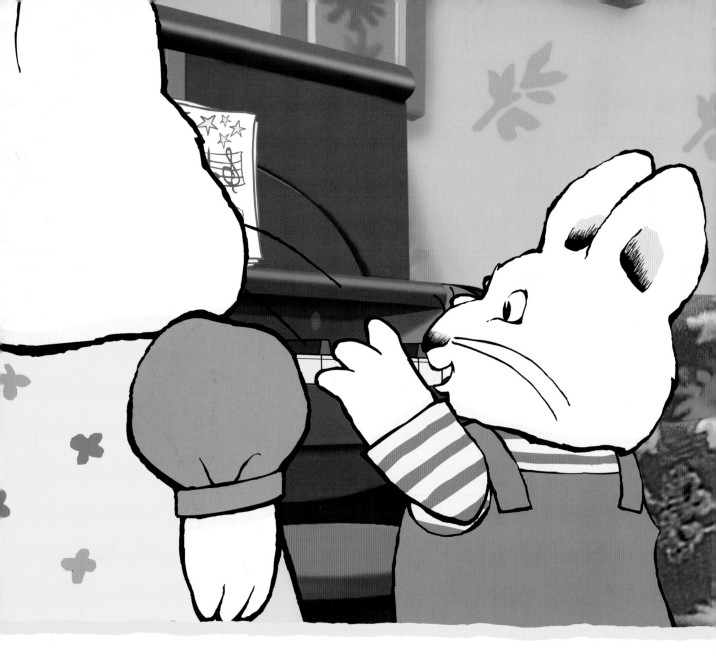

Ruby played the piano. Valerie played the recorder. Louise played the violin.
"Play," said Max. He wanted to play too.

"You don't have a musical instrument,
so you can't make music," said Ruby.

Max still wanted to play, but he didn't have an instrument.
Then he got an idea.

Max ran to his tool box and grabbed a hammer.
"Play," said Max.

Ruby's Red Hot Trio started to play "The Farmer in the Dell."
Suddenly, there was a loud banging sound. It was Max!
"Play," said Max.

"I'm sorry, Max," said Ruby. "It's Ruby's Red Hot Trio.
That means three musicians, not four."
"Four is a quartet," explained Louise.

"Play," said Max, banging with his hammer.
He still wanted to play!

"Please stop making noise, Max," said Ruby.
"We're making music. Tools do not make music."

Max still wanted to play, but he didn't have an instrument.
Then he got an idea.

Max ran to his tool box and grabbed a jackhammer.
"Play," said Max.

Ruby's Red Hot Trio started to play "The Farmer in the Dell" again.
Suddenly, there was a hammering sound. It was Max!
"Play," said Max.

"Please stop making noise, Max," said Ruby.
"We're making music.
Tools do not make music."

Max still wanted to play, but he didn't have another instrument.
Then he got an idea.

Max ran to his tool box and grabbed another hammer
and his Whack-A-Mole toy. "Play," said Max.

Ruby's Red Hot Trio started to play "The Farmer in the Dell" again.
Suddenly, there was a strange sound.
"What's that noise?" asked Valerie.
This time it wasn't Max.

It was Ruby, Valerie and Louise!
They couldn't play the song together.
"How are we ever going to be ready for the
Bunny Scout Concert?" asked Louise.

Then Ruby got an idea.
"I'll tap my foot. You can both follow the beat," said Ruby.
Ruby tapped her foot. Valerie and Louise started to play.

"We sound awful!" said Louise.
"I can't watch your foot and play
at the same time," said Valerie.

"Let's try again," said Ruby.
Ruby's Red Hot Trio started to play "The Farmer in the Dell" again.
Suddenly there was a loud squishy noise.
"Max!" said Ruby. "What are you doing?"

"Wait," said Valerie.
"It's working," said Louise.
"Keep going, Max!" said Ruby.

The girls played "The Farmer in the Dell" again and followed Max's beat.
"That was perfect!" said Louise.
"We'll have to change our name to Ruby's Red Hot Quartet!" said Ruby.
"Featuring Ruby on the piano."

"Louise on the violin," said Louise.
"Valerie on the recorder," said Valerie.
"And Max on the Whack-A-Mole,"
said Ruby, Louise and Valerie together.

"Music!" said Max, playing his Whack-A-Mole again.